Halloween at Glosser's

By Robert Jeschonek

Pie Press

On the night before Halloween, a seance occurs at Glosser Bros...

"Bobby." Erin's voice, when she spoke, was a whisper. "We always said, whichever one of us died first would come back on the night of that person's birthday...right here, at our favorite place, behind Glosser's Department Store." Her heart was beating so fast, she had to pause and take a breath to keep going. "Well, I know it's a long way from Vietnam, but here I am. It's your birthday, the night before Halloween, and I'm right here, Bobby. And I need to talk to you." Her whisper grew fainter. "I need to *see* you."

She waited, her senses keenly focused on the Ouija board, but it didn't budge.

Heart pounding in her chest, she tried again. "Bobby, just answer yes or no. Are you here with me?"

Still, there wasn't the slightest movement from the pointer on the board, or anything else for that matter. Even the flames of the candles seemed perfectly frozen, standing straight up at attention.

"Talk to me, Bobby!" Tears ran down her face, but she didn't dare take her hands off the Ouija board pointer to wipe them away. "Just say *something* so I know you're all right!"

Just then, a man's voice rose up suddenly out of the night. "Excuse me."

Adrenaline shot through Erin as her head swung up in the direction of the voice...

DEDICATION

To the Glosser family, for making parades
and window decorating contests a big part of
our Halloweens for so many years.

And to Ruby Shaffer, for helping keep the
magic alive.

"Why not make the flower a meat-eater?" asked Mrs. Mulligan. "Give it some blood-drenched fangs. Maybe have a person's foot sticking out of its mouth. *That* would be scary, don't you think?"

Sixteen-year-old Erin Lewis just shrugged at the colorful picture she'd painted on the big front window of the Glosser Bros. Department Store in Johnstown, Pennsylvania. It was supposed to be an entry in the 1970 Halloween window painting contest sponsored by Glosser's, but somehow, it just wasn't shaping up to be winner material.

Happy flowers and beaming butterflies didn't exactly shout "Halloween." Neither did the other elements of Erin's painting.

"You need to do something about that sun up there,

too." Mrs. Mulligan pointed one thick finger at the big, smiling orb in the top right corner of the painting. Its bright yellow color was almost the same as the yellow sweater dress clinging to the art teacher's pudgy body. "Instead of a smile, why not give it a gaping, jagged-toothed maw? Maybe give it some devil horns while you're at it, and some big, maniacal eyes."

Erin sighed and frowned. Her right hand fiddled with the military dog tags that hung from a chain at her throat, turning the cool metal chips between her fingers.

"Look, I'm just trying to help you." Mrs. Mulligan gave Erin's shoulder a squeeze. "You're the best artist at Johnstown High School, but you'll never win a prize if you don't paint something scary, or at least give it a Halloween theme."

Looking right and left, Erin saw other kids her age hard at work painting their own visions on Glosser's big windows. There were vampires, zombies, mummies, ghosts, werewolves, aliens, witches, demons, and all manner of monsters...the usual Halloween-type images. She knew how to draw all that stuff; it wasn't brain surgery.

But she didn't feel like it. It was the day before Halloween, but she wasn't in the mood to paint Halloweeny pictures.

"I know you can do it." Mrs. Mulligan nodded eagerly, and her high, blonde hairdo bobbed. "Remember, carnivorous flowers and a demonic sun."

"I don't think so." Looking down, Erin noticed a spot of yellow paint on her olive drab Army-style t-shirt. At least she had a dozen more of them at home. If any paint had gotten on her Army camouflage pants, she couldn't see it among the gray and brown splotches of fabric.

"This is only your second try," said the teacher. "And hey, it's better than your first draft, right? The one with the fluffy bunnies and kittens?"

"I don't want to work on it anymore," said Erin. "I'm done with this one."

"Then how about starting over? Third time's the charm, right?" Mrs. Mulligan grabbed a big brush from a tray on a nearby ladder. "Paint over what you've got there and show us something better suited to the holiday."

Erin's short brown pigtails flicked back and forth on her shoulders as she shook her head slowly. "Maybe I should just quit."

"Not yet." Mrs. Mulligan leaned close and locked her gaze with Erin's. "Just give it one more try, honey, okay?"

Erin recognized the tone of deep concern and encouragement. She'd heard it many times in the past year, ever since the Bad Thing had happened.

She knew it was well-intentioned. Other people were just trying to help by showing sympathy for her loss and giving her a little special treatment.

So why did it still make her want to kick over a couple of paint cans and run away?

"Come on, Erin." The teacher pressed the big brush toward her. "Show us what you can do. Bring home that first prize and make us all proud."

"Okay." Erin took the brush. She would give it another try, though she knew in her heart it would just be another waste of time.

"Great." Mrs. Mulligan grinned. "I can't wait to see what you come up with."

With that, the teacher marched off, pulling a pack of cigarettes out of a pocket in her dress as she headed across the street to Central Park.

Leaving Erin to sigh, then dunk the brush in a can of white paint and slap the start of a fresh coat over the flowers and butterflies on the window.

*****

"What'll it be, sweetie?" The little brown-haired woman in the red smock smiled behind the soda fountain counter in the Glosser Bros. Department Store Cafeteria. "The usual?"

Erin nodded. "Yes, please, Ruby. One chocolate milkshake."

"And what else?" Ruby's kind smile widened, and her eyebrows lifted. "Should I make it a double?"

"No thanks." Erin didn't smile back. It just showed how bad her mood was, that one of her favorite people couldn't cheer her up.

Ruby and her sister Ruth had been there for Erin since she was a little girl, the first time she'd lived in Johnstown. She'd moved to Ohio with her mom and brother six years ago, then had come back to Johnstown one year ago after the Bad Thing happened. She'd needed friends more than ever at that point, and had picked up right where she'd left off with Ruby and Ruth. It was good having some supportive adult friends, since Mom was still a mess from the Bad Thing, and Erin's father had never been in the picture from the beginning.

"Here you go." Ruby lowered her voice to a whisper as she handed over the chocolate shake. "And I gave you something extra, after all."

Looking down at the shake, Erin saw it had three maraschino cherries on top instead of just one. It was enough to get a small smile out of her at last. "Thanks, Ruby." She reached over with two dollar bills to pay for the shake.

"On the house." Ruby wouldn't take the cash. "So what's got you down, anyway?"

ROBERT JESCHONEK

Erin sighed. "I'm disqualified from the window-painting contest. My paintings weren't scary enough."

Ruby shook her head. "They just threw you out?"

"They gave me three chances." Erin thought of her third painting, which had turned out to be the stylized face of the lady from the ads for the Gee Bee stores (also owned by Glosser Bros.), smiling at a basket of puppies. "Three strikes, and I'm out."

Ruby picked up a parfait glass and polished it with a white rag. "I'll bet they were all wonderful." She leaned forward across the counter. "It's their loss, disqualifying you like that."

"Thanks." Erin sipped the shake through her straw. It was delicious as always.

"You can come and paint *my* windows," said Ruby. "I'd love anything you paint."

"Thanks, Ruby." Erin sipped some more shake.

"I'll bet there are lots of people who appreciate you," said Ruby. "People who make you feel better instead of worse."

Erin smiled. One other person did come to mind, one person beside Ruby and Ruth who might help her feel better.

Maybe now was a good time to go see her.

*****

"More slime over here! And somebody get me another bucket of blood!"

When Erin walked her ten-speed bicycle into the big garage where the Halloween float was taking shape, her best friend Donna's voice was the first thing she heard. It was a big voice, impossible to ignore, much like the girl it belonged to.

As soon as Erin walked into view, that voice was aimed point-blank at her. "Hey, wait a second! Did somebody order a creature from the black lagoon?"

Erin's mood still sucked, but she smiled anyway. "Hi, Donna."

"Get outta here!" Donna hurried over and shooed her toward the door. "Tell them to send us the Bride of Frankenstein we ordered!"

"They're fresh out." Erin shrugged as she leaned her bike against the wall. "I guess you'll have to settle for me."

Donna, who was six feet tall and played on Johnstown's varsity girls' basketball team, glared down at her in mock disgust. "We'll just have to make do, then. Come on and I'll drape some fake intestines over you."

"I'll bet you say that to all your friends," said Erin.

Donna smirked. "You know I do." She brushed her dirty hands on her mismatched sweats--red top, black pants--which were covered in paint smears, sawdust, and glitter. Her long, black hair, which was tied in a ponytail, was full of the same stuff. "So what brings you to this *neck* of the woods, as Dracula might say? I thought you were painting windows."

"Not anymore," said Erin. "I got disqualified."

"Good!" Donna spun and headed for the float-in-progress, where two younger girls were hard at work with paint brushes. "I could use another pair of hands around here!"

As Erin followed, she took a closer look at the float, which consisted of a red base on a four-wheeled flatbed surrounded by cut-out waist-high flames of red, orange, and yellow. The girls' basketball teams were putting it together, using a spare bay at Donna's father's auto repair center.

"So what's this going to be, then?" asked Erin.

"It's Hell, baby!" Donna threw her arms in the air dramatically. "A *special* Hell for the people of Johnstown! We're gonna have Morley's Devil-Dog poking people with a pitchfork, and Mr. Flood dumping buckets of water on the crowd, wearing a powder-blue leisure suit!"

"Buckets of water?" Erin fiddled with the dog tags. "Won't that make people mad?"

"Okay, okay," said Donna. "Buckets of confetti, then."

"I like it," said Erin. "Maybe you could have a steel mill

demon pouring make-believe hot metal on the damned. Or an Inclined Plane torture rack that keeps going up and down, like it's crushing them to a pulp."

"Yes!" Donna jabbed a finger in Erin's direction. "Perfect! And *that's* why I need your help! You've got that sick creativity, Eerie!"

Erin waved at one of the girls who was painting the base of the float--a redhead and cousin of Donna's from the jayvee girls' basketball squad. The girl smiled and waved back. "Well, I don't know what good it'll do your float. You might be better off without me."

"Why would you think that?" asked Donna. "Sick creativity is *always* a good thing."

"Not lately, it isn't." Erin watched as the other girl, a blonde who was also a jayvee basketball player, mixed a big bucket of some kind of slimy green goo. "My window painting sure didn't come out very sick."

"Why?" Donna went to work shaping a wire frame that looked like it might be the skeleton of a papier-mache boulder. "What did you paint?"

"Bunnies and kittens," said Erin. "Flowers and puppies. And the Gee Bee lady."

Donna laughed. "I love it! You were totally rebelling against the system! Breaking the rules to stick it to the man!"

"Not really."

"Then you were making a statement!" said Donna. "An artistic or political statement!"

Erin shook her head. "That's not it, either."

Donna stopped working on the wire frame and looked up at her. "Then what gives, Eerie?"

"I just..." Erin frowned. "I just couldn't do it."

"Okay." A look of sympathy flashed across Donna's paint-speckled face, quickly replaced by a sarcastic smile. She, more than just about anyone, understood where Erin was coming from and what the Bad Thing meant to her. They'd been friends since the first time Erin had lived in town, six years ago, and they both knew everything about each other. "Then I say, get back on the horse." She gestured at a pile of Styrofoam heads, the kind department stores used to display wigs for sale. "Start painting those disembodied heads, wouldja? Make 'em nice and gruesome, and stick 'em on those pikes for the gates of Hell."

"Okay." Erin still didn't feel like she could do the job right, but she thought she'd give it a try.

"Now get cracking!" Donna clapped her hands loudly. "Hell wasn't built in a day, y'know!"

*****

It was well after dark by the time Erin walked through

the door of the Hornerstown apartment she shared with her mother...late enough to earn her a scolding for missing dinner.

In the old days, that is. The days before the Bad Thing happened.

Now, Mom wasn't even home. The lights were off, and the place was quiet as a tomb. Which, considering the way things were going, was very appropriate.

Erin slammed the door behind her and flicked the switch for the living room light...but nothing happened. "Great." She tried again with the same result.

The same thing happened when she tried turning on the TV. Sadly, it wasn't a surprise. It wasn't the first time Mom had forgotten (or been unable) to pay the electric bill. There were lots of things she didn't take care of anymore.

Not that Erin really blamed her. The Bad Thing had hit Mom worse than anyone, and it hadn't happened that long ago. A single mother, she'd moved back to Johnstown, where she and the kids had lived until six years ago--anything to make a change. But it hadn't helped much. She was still a wreck, and Erin was enough of a mess herself that she hadn't been able to help her heal. It was totally understandable that she was still struggling, trying to deal with it by drinking a little too much and staying out a little too late.

Totally understandable.

With a sigh, Erin kicked off her combat boots and padded out to the kitchen. She ate a few Ritz crackers dipped in peanut butter--just enough to stop her stomach from growling--and washed them down with grape Kool Aid.

Then, she ducked through a doorway around the corner into her bedroom. Getting down on her knees, she slid a beat-up black backpack out from under the bed and took a moment to go through the contents by the glow of the streetlight outside her window.

At a glance, it looked like everything was there... everything she needed for her mission that night. Four candles, matches, a flashlight...

...incense, an incense burner, a little brass bowl...

...a Ouija board and planchette pointer...

...three baseball cards...

...a lock of hair from her dead brother, Bobby...

...and a letter he'd written long ago.

All set.

Erin zipped up the backpack and pulled it over her shoulders, then paused before getting to her feet. Without warning, a tear formed in the corner of her left eye, then rolled down her cheek.

And she stopped it, swiping it away with the back of her hand.

"Come on." She took a deep breath and released it

slowly, fighting to keep more tears from falling. It shouldn't be a problem, she knew.

Tonight wasn't an occasion for sadness, was it? It was a night for joy.

After all, she was about to see someone she hadn't seen in quite some time. She was about to see her big brother, Bobby, who'd died in Vietnam a year ago.

That was what the Bad Thing had been--Bobby's death in the war at the age of 19. And getting to see him again was the only thing that had kept her going since it happened. Knowing it was coming soon had been the only thing keeping her sane.

Though three years apart in age, the two of them had always been close. They'd done everything together, at least until he'd been drafted and gone off to boot camp. Even then, all the way to Vietnam, he'd stayed in touch faithfully, sending her lots of letters. Then, the letters had stopped, and the news of his death had come soon after.

In the year since then, she'd been heartsick, counting down the days until she could see him again...until the agreement they'd made as kids could be fulfilled.

Now, finally, tonight was the night. Was it any wonder she'd been distracted at Glosser's window painting contest and not much better at the garage decorating the float with Donna?

Jumping to her feet, she hurried out of the room. She pulled on her combat boots and rushed out the front door, slamming it shut on her way to what she was sure would be the first happy night she'd known in months.

*****

Erin was breathing hard as she rode her ten-speed into the alley between the main building of the Glosser Bros. Department Store and the annex that housed the cafeteria. She was pretty sure no one had seen her; it was after 11 o'clock, so town was pretty quiet, and there hadn't been any traffic on Franklin Street when she'd turned down the alley.

The store and cafeteria had been closed for hours, and the windows were all dark. When she got to the end of the alley, she saw that the loading dock area located there was dark, too.

Stopping the bike to listen, she didn't hear any telltale sounds of anyone lurking nearby. Reaching into the backpack, she pulled out the flashlight and shone its beam into the shadowy corners of the dock area, but saw no one.

Perfect. It was just the way she'd hoped it would be.

Dismounting the bike, Erin parked it against a wall. Then, she proceeded to walk the last few steps to the middle of the open space around the loading dock, framed by the back of the Glosser Building and the buildings behind it along Washington Street.

Looking down, she saw a red X spray-painted on the pavement. "Right here." It marked the exact spot where the ritual would take place. She and Bobby had put it there six years ago, when this had been their favorite hiding place during their explorations around town.

Sitting cross-legged beside the X, facing Glosser's loading dock, she unloaded her backpack and set up her tools. The Ouija board went over the X. She lit a votive candle at each of the board's four corners, then set up the incense burner at the top edge. She loaded the burner with a stick of Nag Champa incense and lit that, too.

Finally, she was ready. Taking a deep, shaky breath, she held up one of the baseball cards. One of *Bobby's* baseball cards--Willie Mays of the San Francisco Giants.

"Bobby, I'm here." She lit the card with a match and watched as it burned. When it was almost down to her fingertips, she dropped it in the little brass bowl and let it burn the rest of the way to ash.

Then, she set fire to another card--Roberto Clemente of the Pittsburgh Pirates, Bobby's all-time favorite player. "I'm here, just like we said." Again, she let it burn to ash in the brass bowl.

She burned one more card after that--Catfish Hunter of

the Oakland A's. Then she lit the lock of Bobby's hair and dropped that in the bowl, too.

Next, she reached for the letter and read it for what must have been the ten thousandth time. And then she pressed it to her chest and closed her eyes.

"Bobby." Her voice, when she spoke, was a whisper. "We always said, whichever one of us died first would come back on the night of that person's birthday...right here, at our favorite place, behind Glosser's." Her heart was beating so fast, she had to pause and take a breath to keep going. "Well, I know it's a long way from Vietnam, but here I am. It's your birthday, the night before Halloween, and I'm right here, Bobby. And I need to talk to you." Her whisper grew fainter. "I need to *see* you."

Just then, a car whooshed by on the street, breaking her mood...but only for a moment. She closed her eyes again and continued whispering. "So here goes, Bobby. Just the way we talked about it...before you went to Vietnam. Just the way we agreed it would be."

Erin folded the letter once and put it on her lap. Leaning forward, she took the glass planchette from her backpack and placed it on the Ouija board. Then, she rested her fingertips lightly on the planchette, careful not to apply too much pressure.

"Okay, Bobby," she said. "Let's start with a question.

Are you here?"

She waited, her senses keenly focused on the planchette, but it didn't budge.

Heart pounding in her chest, she tried again. "Bobby, just answer yes or no. Are you here with me?"

Still, there wasn't the slightest movement from the planchette, or anything else for that matter. Even the flames of the candles seemed perfectly frozen, pointing straight up at attention.

Erin waited a little longer, but it was hard. She'd already waited so long, and now she was *right here*, at the appointed time and place, and she needed to see her brother so badly. She needed to tell him how much she missed him, and how sorry she was that she'd never said goodbye, and how Mom was falling apart without him. Most of all, she needed him to make her *feel better* somehow, like she wasn't always about to shatter into a million pieces even as she walked around pretending she was fine.

But none of that was happening yet. The planchette remained steady, as if glued to the board.

"Bobby, please," said Erin. "Why won't you talk to me?"

Still nothing. How many times had she and Bobby played with the Ouija board, and they'd always gotten some kind of response, no matter how slight? But now, when she needed it the most, there was nothing.

17

"Talk to me, Bobby!" Tears ran down her face, but she didn't dare take her hands off the planchette to wipe them away. "Just say *something* so I know you're all right!"

Just then, a man's voice rose up suddenly out of the night. "Excuse me."

Adrenaline shot through Erin as her head swung up in the direction of the voice.

"Are you all right?" The man, who'd come down the alley, stepped into the moonlight so she could see him.

Instantly, a tidal wave of disappointment rushed through her. The guy wasn't Bobby. He was a hippie, and he didn't look or sound anything like him.

Instead of short, brown hair, he had long, blond hair. Instead of a broad-shouldered, muscular frame in Army fatigues, he had a scrawny, knobby body in a suede fringe jacket, white v-neck t-shirt, and torn jeans. Instead of a strong, deep voice, he had a raspy, gravelly one.

And he wore glasses, wire frames. Bobby had had perfect vision until the day he'd died. Not to mention, the hippie was carrying a bottle in a bag...and Bobby never drank.

"Yes, I'm fine." Erin scrambled to her feet and dusted herself off. "Thanks for asking."

"So what'cha doin'?" The hippie frowned a little as he stared at the Ouija board, candles, and incense. "Trying to channel the ghosts of the original Glosser Brothers?"

Erin shook her head, feeling suddenly self-conscious, embarrassed...and also a little worried about being alone with a strange guy at a deserted loading dock around twelve o'clock midnight.

"Hey, it's cool if you are." The hippie put his hands up in front of him, one still holding the bottle in the bag. "It's groovy. Whatever floats your boat, I always say."

"I'm trying to contact my brother." The words rushed out of her by surprise, before she could call them back. "He died in Vietnam a year ago."

Slowly, the hippie lowered his hands. "So how's it going? Any luck?" He gestured at the Ouija board setup.

"No," said Erin. "Nothing."

"Damn." The hippie wagged his shaggy head. "Maybe he just can't cross over, y'know? Maybe he really wants to, but he can't."

Erin shrugged. "I guess."

The hippie swigged whatever was in the bottle in the bag, then wiped his mouth on the sleeve of his jacket. "Or maybe he's already come to see you, and you just didn't know it. Maybe you just didn't recognize him."

Erin frowned, considering what he'd said. "I hadn't thought of that."

"So what do you want from him anyway?" asked the hippie. "What do you expect? Some kind'a message, maybe?"

"I guess so," said Erin.

The hippie smiled and sipped from the bottle again. "Well, what if it was you, talkin' from the other side? What kind of message would you send if you could?"

Erin thought for a moment. "I don't know. 'Don't worry,' maybe? 'Everything will be okay?'"

"Okay, good," said the hippie. "You know what mine would be? 'Peace.' That's all. Just 'peace,' man."

"'Peace.'" Erin narrowed her eyes. "What kind of peace?"

"Every kind." The hippie spread his arms wide. "*All* kinds. Peace for everyone, everywhere, in every way." Lowering his arms, he started to back away down the alley. "What better message could there be, huh?"

With that, he gave her a two-fingered peace symbol salute. As he turned and shuffled off into the shadows, Erin saw the cartoon face of the lady from the Gee Bee ads on the back of his suede jacket. She couldn't help smiling; the whole time she'd been talking to him, she hadn't even known it was there.

Then, he was gone, leaving her alone in the moonlight again.

Erin stood there for a while, thinking about what he'd said. What if he was right, and Bobby had already come back? After all, he would've done everything in his power to keep his solemn promise to her. What if she just hadn't recognized him?

Lost in thought, Erin slowly sat down at the Ouija board...then suddenly sprang to her feet. "Oh my God." Heart hammering, she ran down the alley and out onto Franklin Street, looking for the hippie.

But he was gone.

Erin ran up the block and turned the corner of Washington Street, but saw no sign of him there. Then, she ran back down the block and around the corner of Locust Street, again to no avail.

She ran through Central Park, too, looking behind every tree and monument. She bolted onto Main Street and peered in both directions, looking for that suede fringe jacket with the Gee Bee lady's face on the back.

And finding nothing. The hippie was gone.

Or was he ever a hippie in the first place? What if he'd been someone else in disguise all along?

"Oh, Bobby." She couldn't prove it. He'd said nothing, in fact, to lead her to think it was true. She might live her whole life forever wondering, never knowing for certain if that had been him.

But for now, for tonight, when she needed it most, she chose to believe.

And that meant taking his message to heart, didn't it?

"Peace." Fingering the dog tags at her throat--*his* dog tags, Bobby's dog tags--she considered the word. Wondered what it might mean to her.

Peace of mind, maybe...finally accepting that Bobby was gone and learning to move on. But there was more to it, wasn't there? *Peace for everyone, everywhere, in every way.* That's what the hippie had said.

So what exactly could she do with that?

By the time she'd walked back to the loading dock behind Glosser's, she knew. She knew exactly what she wanted to do with that message.

"Thank you, Bobby." She blew out one candle, then another. "Thank you for keeping your promise. And thank you for sending me a message."

Then, she blew out the third candle. "Now wait till you see what I do about it." And then she blew out the fourth candle, too.

*****

Early the next morning--Halloween morning--Erin skidded her bike into the parking lot in front of Donna's father's garage. She hopped off and let it fall to the pavement without a second thought, in too much of a hurry to worry about leaning it against a wall.

The garage door was up, but she didn't see anyone inside. It was just after eight, so it was possible the float-making team hadn't arrived yet.

"Donna?" As Erin walked into the garage, her eyes went straight to the big, red float. It looked closer to being finished than it had the day before, with lots of papier-mache boulders scattered around and a hellish altar draped in a red tablecloth in the middle. The "gates of Hell" were done, too--poles at the front corners of the float, spiked with the Styrofoam heads she'd decorated. Each head was painted with gruesome features and had patches of hair and rubber insects stapled in place. They looked pretty good, she thought, though she hadn't been at her best when she'd worked on them.

"Hey there, Eerie." Donna strolled out from behind the float with a steaming Styrofoam cup in her hand. "Welcome back to Hell."

Erin smiled. "I feel like I never left."

"Coffee?" Donna raised her cup.

"Yes, please," said Erin. "I didn't get much sleep last night."

Donna narrowed her eyes suspiciously. "And why is that, young lady?"

"There was something I had to take care of," said Erin.

Donna cocked her head to one side. "What was his

name, pray tell?"

"Nothing like that." Erin brushed a hand through the air. "More like...trying to find someone I hadn't heard from in a long time."

"And did you?" asked Donna.

"I don't know. Maybe." Erin shrugged. "It's complicated."

"If you say so." Donna turned and walked around the back of the float, leading Erin to a coffeemaker set up on a dirty, cluttered workbench. She filled a Styrofoam cup with the steaming black brew from the pot and handed it to Erin, then topped off her own cup. "I'm just glad you're here. The girls who were helping me called in late, so I could use the help."

Erin sipped the bitter black coffee and bobbed her head toward the float. "Looks like you're almost done."

"I wish." Donna rolled her eyes. "I've still got a *ton* to do."

"Oh yeah?" Erin had another sip. "So, uh...I guess you wouldn't mind a little *redesign* then?"

Donna's expression instantly turned into a scowl. "What *kind* of redesign?"

Cup in hand, Erin walked over to the float. "Oh, you know. A little tweak here, a little tweak there."

"How *many* tweaks?"

Erin cleared her throat. "All of them."

"*All* of them?"

"Yeah, you know." Erin spread her arms wide. "Everything."

"*Everything?*"

"Pretty much."

"Are you *crazy?* We have to be in line by 6:00 for the parade tonight!"

"I know," said Erin. "But it'll be great. It's the best idea ever."

Donna stormed over, spilling coffee from the rim of her cup, and landed in front of Erin. "We don't have *time*, Erin!"

"But it's my sick creativity, remember?" Erin grinned. "You said you love it."

"I do, but we can't do this! It's just too late!"

"No it's not," said Erin. "I know exactly how we can make it work. Trust me."

"But I...but we..."

"Trust me." Erin reached over and laid her hand on Donna's shoulder. "This will be the best float in the parade by far. The best float *ever.*"

"But Johnstown Hell was gonna be great! What about Morley's Demon Dog? What about Mr. Flood throwing buckets of water at the crowd?"

"That would've been great, too," said Erin. "But people will *never* forget this float. Trust me."

At that, Donna scrunched her eyes shut and let loose a cry of frustration. "This is nuts!"

"Donna, please." Erin gave her friend's shoulder a squeeze. "I need to do this. It's important."

"Gah!" Donna shook her head hard. "I can't believe I'm doing this!" She opened her eyes. "All right, Eerie! You win! But this better be as great as you say, or I swear to God I'll *murderize* you!"

"It will be," said Erin. "Now here's what we need to do..."

*****

That night, not long after dark, the Fifth Annual Glosser Bros. Halloween Parade made its way up Main Street in downtown Johnstown. The sidewalks and curbs were packed with hundreds of spectators, crowding in for a look at the marching bands and Halloween-themed floats...crowding in also to catch some of the treats that were being thrown from the goodie bags of passing masqueraders.

Little did they know it, but they were in for something very different in the middle of the parade. That was where the float that Erin had redesigned was located, smack between the Windber High School marching band and a troop of boy scouts dressed up like Indians.

The float didn't look like much at first, though. Set up on the flatbed towed by Donna's dad's pickup, it was nowhere near as lively as the other floats that came before it. No one was waving at the crowd or throwing candy or acting out a skit. It was almost like no one was aboard the float at all, like the crew hadn't bothered to show up.

But they were there, all right. Erin, Donna, and half the varsity and jayvee girls' basketball squads were up there, hunkered down amid the abundant greenery that covered the flatbed.

Just as Erin had envisioned, the float was completely different from its original concept. Instead of a barren, red-slathered Hell surrounded by flames, it had become a jungle, piled with simulated (and not-so-simulated) vegetation.

The fiery cutouts around the edges had been wrapped in a tangle of leafy vines and limbs. Two palm trees stood at the rear, brown papier-mache trunks topped with green-painted cardboard fronds. Down the middle, there were heaps of freshly-cut brush, piled together like little hills.

The only things remaining from the original design were the poles spiked with gruesome Styrofoam heads, one at each corner of the front of the flatbed.

The float rolled up Main Street for a few blocks, getting

plenty of puzzled stares and comments from the crowd. What was it supposed to be? Why wasn't there anyone aboard? Why wasn't there a sign at least, so people would know who'd sponsored it?

But for a while, no explanations were forthcoming. The float just glided along, still and silent, as spectators complained and made fun of it.

Then, when it got to Central Park, the float stopped in the street. The parade behind it had no choice but to stop there, too.

That's when Donna's dad pushed the 8-track tape into the player in the cab of his truck and hit the play button.

Suddenly, "War, What Is It Good For?" by Edwin Starr came blasting out of the pickup's windows.

That was the cue Erin had been waiting for. As the music played, she popped up from under one of the piles of brush on the flatbed, dressed in a combat uniform straight out of Vietnam, complete with helmet and toy rifle from Glosser's Halloween costume department.

Turning slowly, she surveyed her surroundings as if she were in the jungle. She looked left, then right, keeping her rifle raised at all times.

Then, when her back was turned, Donna popped up from under the brush behind her. She was dressed the same way (courtesy of the clearance racks at the Army Navy Store up the street) except her helmet had "VC" painted on it in white letters...and she also had a toy rifle, which she swung up and pretended to fire.

Erin lunged forward as if she'd been shot, then dropped to the flatbed. Meanwhile, another girl in combat gear from the Army Navy Store, this one with a "US" helmet, popped up and pretended to fire at Donna, who also went down.

One after another, the varsity and jayvee girls--half with "US" helmets, half with "VC"--popped up and fell down before make-believe gunshots, until no one was left. For a moment, they all stayed down, concealed in the foliage, as the music continued to blare.

Then, one by one, they rose up--only now they had no guns and were wearing ghoulish, glow-in-the-dark green masks. Groaning loudly, they shambled around the float like zombies with their arms extended.

The music reached a crescendo and stopped, and so did the zombies. They stayed like that, frozen, as the next song started playing in the truck. It was "Imagine" by John Lennon.

Rain started to fall as the zombie soldiers all joined hands and sang along. It was just as Erin had imagined it, a perfect ending to get across the message that the hippie in the alley had given her.

"How'd I let you talk me into this?" whispered Donna.

"It's about the corniest thing ever."

Erin didn't care. All that mattered was that she felt like she'd done something good for Bobby, something he would've loved if he'd seen it.

Not that everyone in the crowd appreciated it, though. Lots of people glared and booed and waved dismissively at the float. Some even stomped off angrily into the night. They didn't seem to understand what Erin was trying to say--that in death, everyone's the same, no matter which side they're on. Imagine if enemies could realize that before killing each other; maybe good men like Bobby wouldn't have to die. That's what Erin was saying.

She wasn't really taking a stand against the war or the people who were in favor of it. She was against what it had done to her brother and so many other people's loved ones. She was against letting it happen again.

She thought it was a good message, even if so many people in the crowd were against it. But the good news was, they weren't all like that. Some people--younger ones, mostly, but some older ones, too--were even singing along.

That included Erin's friends, Ruby and Ruth Shaffer. They were right there in the front of the crowd in their coats and babushkas, smiling and waving excitedly at Erin.

And all of them were there together in that moment in the rain, listening to John Lennon singing about a different world while the lights of the Glosser Bros. Department Store glowed softly through the red-and-gold-leafed trees of Central Park.

ROBERT JESCHONEK

Glosser's Halloween Photo Gallery

Window painting photos by Ruby Shaffer (unless marked otherwise).

Parade photos courtesy of William Glosser.

Photo from Glosser Bros. Annual Report, Jan. 1976

Photo courtesy of William Glosser

ABOUT THE AUTHOR

Robert Jeschonek is an award-winning writer whose fiction, comics, essays, articles, and podcasts have been published around the world. His books about Johnstown, Pennsylvania include the fictional tales *Christmas At Glosser's* and *Easter At Glosser's* and the non-fiction histories *Long Live Glosser's* and *Penn Traffic Forever.* He has also written *Star Trek* and *Doctor Who* fiction and *Batman* and *Justice Society* comics. His young adult fantasy novel, *My Favorite Band Does Not Exist,* won the Forward National Literature Award and was named a Top Ten First Novel for Youth by *Booklist.* His cross-genre science fiction thriller, *Day 9,* is an International Book Award winner. He also won the Scribe Award for Best Original Novel from the International Association of Media Tie-in Writers for his alternate history, *Tannhäuser: Rising Sun, Falling Shadows.* He was nominated for the British Fantasy Award for his story, "Fear of Rain." Visit him online at www.robertjeschonek.com. You can also find him on Facebook and follow him as @TheFictioneer on Twitter.

ANOTHER GREAT JOHNSTOWN STORY NOW AVAILABLE FROM ROBERT JESCHONEK

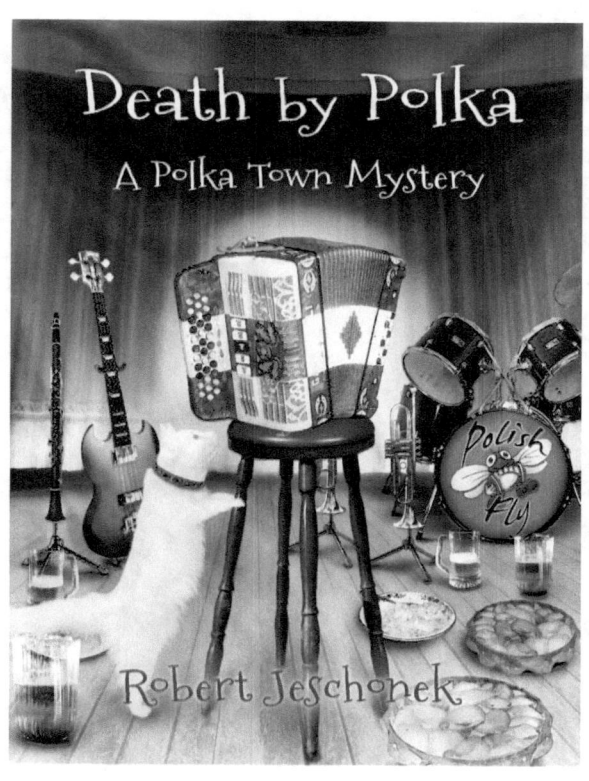

DEATH
BY
POLKA

BY ROBERT JESCHONEK

Who killed Polish Lou, the famous Prince of Polka Music? His daughter, musicologist Lottie Kachowski, comes home to the polka heartland of Johnstown, Pennsylvania, to find the answer. Lottie has an unbeatable talent for using music to solve crimes, and she does just that on the trail of her father's killer. But the stakes turn deadlier than ever when another polka legend comes to a tragic end. As the danger rises, Lottie recruits her father's wacky girlfriend, Polish Peg, to help her dig deeper into the wild world of small town polka. At the same time, she fights to keep from getting dragged back into the polka scene she left behind long ago.

AND NOW, A SPECIAL PREVIEW OF DEATH BY POLKA...

As I looked out over the crowd in the banquet hall, the Furies glared back at me in disgust. There were three of them, all dressed in black, all with raven black hair, and they were my sisters.

Bonnie, the oldest and tallest, stood in the middle. Her brown eyes framed a big, angular nose that gave her the look of a hawk. Her hair was long, draped over her shoulders, but not nearly as long as mine.

Charlie stood at her side. She was shorter and rounder than any of us, with plump cheeks and dark blue eyes. Her hair was cut in a kind of dowdy helmet 'do that made her look older than she was, older than any of us.

Then there was Ellie, the youngest. She looked like an anorexic teen, all skin and bones and giant blue eyes so pale they were almost white. Those eyes peering out from her shag haircut with the spiky bangs looked perpetually challenging, always ready to go off.

Which, actually, described her personality. All *three* of the Furies' personalities.

Boy did they have capital "T" tempers. They were always, *always* fighting with each other, shifting alliances, holding grudges on top of grudges.

But today, for once, they were united against a common object of resentment. *Me*, in other words. I had the honor of having brought them together in harmony. I could see it in their body language as they all clustered together and stared up at me through slitted eyes. I could feel it in the air, and I could guess what had brought it on.

They were mad that I was the only sister called up on stage. It didn't matter that I didn't *want* to be there; I knew my sisters, and I *knew* this was eating them alive.

It was just the latest in a series of injustices. First, I'd gone off to Los Angeles while they'd all stayed in town and given birth to the ADHD Dozen. Then, I'd gotten engaged, while the best they'd been able to manage was a string of deadbeat baby daddies. Now this.

I knew I'd pay for it later, but I chose to ignore them for now. Basil Sloveski was waving a number ten white business envelope over his giant silver pompadour.

"All right, folks!" The corners of Basil's eyes crinkled as

he grinned. Up close, I could see his whole overtanned face was a web of fine lines. "Without further ado!"

The crowd roared (except for the Furies, who just rolled their eyes) and pumped beers in the air. The ADHD Dozen squirmed their way up front and lined up along the stage, screeching and dancing like idiots.

"How about a drum roll, guys?" When Basil said it, Eddie Sr.'s ancient drummer hopped up on the stage, raised his bony arms in a weight-lifter's pose with fists curled toward his shaggy white head, and dropped down on the squeaky red stool behind his drum kit.

As the drum roll started, Basil slid a fingernail under the corner of the envelope flap, then dragged his nail along the length of the flap, tearing it open with a ripping sound.

My heart pounded, and I held my breath. As badly as I didn't want to be there, I was actually caught up in the suspense. Polish Lou's showmanship had broken through even my tough exterior.

The kids down in front couldn't stand the suspense either. They were hopping up and down, clawing at the stage, having conniptions. Milly spoke for all of them. "*What? What's it say?*"

Basil slipped two tanned fingers into the envelope and drew out a folded sheet of paper. He cleared his throat as he unfolded it, playing up the drama.

Then, he started reading. "Dear fellow polka lovers!" The drum roll continued in the background as Basil's voice rang over the crowd. "As you know, I've been called the Prince of Pennsylvania Polka."

The crowd roared its approval.

"But now that the *Prince* is dead, who will rule his *kingdom?*" Basil paused and looked around the banquet hall for dramatic effect. "Who will be my *successor?*"

"*Who? Who?*" squeaked one of the kids down in front.

"Who will carry on the tradition of great polka music as leader of my band, Polish Fly?" read Basil. "Who will continue to broadcast three hours of polkatacular tunetasticness every Saturday morning and Sunday afternoon on my radio show, *Kocham Taniec?*

"Who will organize the annual Polkapourri festival that has become an institution for Johnstown and the entire tri-state area?

"And who will manage Polish Lou Enterprises now that Polish Lou is gone?" Basil stopped reading aloud, though his eyes kept scanning the page. He got a funny look on his face, a kind of smirking frown, like he wasn't sure he'd read the letter correctly. Then he shrugged, nodded, and gazed out at the crowd. "I'll tell you who!

"*She* will!" With that, Basil swung an arm around and pointed directly at Peg.

4

The drum roll ended with a rim shot, and the crowd cheered like crazy. Eddie Sr. and Eddie Jr. played wild strains on their accordions. In front of the stage, the kids spun and jumped and gyrated like human popcorn in their little suits and dresses.

Glancing at the Furies, I saw the three of them looked more thoroughly disgusted than ever. One thing they all had in common and shared with me was an undying hatred of Polish Peg.

As for the Clown herself, she beamed and waved with pure delight. If I hadn't known any better, I might've thought she'd just won the Miss America pageant or an Academy Award.

Clapping politely, I turned away and looked for the best place to step down from the stage. The crowd was slightly thinner by the corner, so maybe that would be a good exit point.

Just as I took a step toward the corner, Basil called out behind me. "And *she* will, too!"

I swear, everyone in the banquet hall gasped at once. Except me.

"That's right!" said Basil. "I'm talking about *you*, Lottie!"

At the mention of my name, I spun to face him. "Me, what?"

"You're the *co-queen* of Lou's kingdom, that's what!"

Basil lunged over and grabbed my arm, then hauled it high like I'd just won a prize fight. "Ladies and polkamen! Meet the new rulers of Polka Land! Lou's own daughter, Lottie..." Basil grabbed Peg's arm and hefted it overhead alongside mine. "...and his partner, the love of his life, Polish Peg!"

The crowd went berserk. Cameras flashed in my eyes as Eddie Sr. and Eddie Jr. launched into "Hail to the Chief" on their accordions.

Dazed, I leaned forward and looked past Basil at Peg. The look on her clownish face said it all.

She was as surprised as I was. And just about as happy.

Which, let me tell you, wasn't happy at all.

www.ingramcontent.com/pod-product-compliance
Lightning Source LLC
Chambersburg PA
CBHW050905120626
46554CB00003B/1032